Disney · PIXAR

TOY
STORY

Disney's

Aladdin

Disney's THE
LION KING

Disney
CD Storybook

Disney
CD Storybook

The Lion King
The Little Mermaid
Toy Story
Aladdin

Hinkler Books Pty Ltd 2004
45-55 Fairchild Street
Heatherton VIC 3202 Australia
www.hinklerbooks.com

20 19 18 17 16 15 14
10 09 08 07

© Disney Enterprises, Inc.

ISBN 13: 978 1 8651 5304 9
ISBN 10: 1 8651 5304 4

Printed and manuctured in China.

Disney
CD Storybook

Contents

Lion King

Mufasa the Lion King
Roamed far and wide,
Ruling his kingdom
With wisdom and pride.
As king of the land,
He gave all that he had.
To Simba, his cub,
He was just a great dad.

Lion Cub

One, two,
What does Simba do?
Three, four,
He gives a big roar.
Five, six,
He often plays tricks.
Seven, eight,
He lies in wait.
Nine, ten,
He's back in his den!

Every morning, as the sun peeked over the horizon, a giant rock formation caught the first rays of light. This was Pride Rock, home to King Mufasa and his lovely wife, Queen Sarabi.

On this particular morning, animals from all over the Pride Lands had journeyed to Pride Rock to honor the birth of the newborn cub, Simba.

As part of the celebration, Rafiki had a special duty. He cracked open a gourd, dipped his finger inside and made a mark on Simba's forehead. Then Rafiki lifted the future king up high for all to see.

The elephants trumpeted with their trunks, giraffes bowed their heads and the zebras stamped their hooves with approval.

Not far from the ceremony, in a cave at the backside of Pride Rock, a scraggly lion with a dark mane grumbled. "Life's not fair. I shall never be King." This was Mufasa's brother, Scar, who was jealous of Simba's position as the next king.

Moments later, Mufasa was at the doorway to Scar's cave. "Sarabi and I didn't see you at the presentation of Simba," he said.

Zazu, Mufasa's trusted advisor, also appeared. "You should have been first in line," he said. "I was first in line until the little hairball was born," Scar replied. And with that, he stalked out of the cave.

Before long, Simba grew into a healthy, playful young cub. Early one morning, he and Mufasa climbed to the top of Pride Rock. As they looked out at the rising sun, Mufasa pointed across the Pride Lands. "Look, Simba: Everything the light touches is our kingdom."

Simba scanned the horizon and noticed a dark spot in the distance. "What about that shadowy place?"

"That's beyond our borders. You must never go there, Simba," said Mufasa.

"But I thought a king can do whatever he wants," Simba said.

"There's more to being king than getting your way all the time," said Mufasa. "Everything you see exists together in a delicate balance. As king you need to understand that balance and respect all the creatures—from the crawling ant to the leaping antelope. We are all connected in the great Circle of Life."

Later, as Simba headed back down the path, he ran into Scar. "Hey, Uncle Scar! Guess what? I'm gonna be King of Pride Rock. My dad just showed me the whole kingdom! And I'm gonna rule it all!"

Scar looked slyly at the young cub. "He didn't show you what's beyond that rise at the northern border?"

"Well, no. He said I can't go there," said Simba.

"And he's absolutely right. It's far too dangerous," said Scar. "Only the bravest lions go there. Promise me you'll never visit that dreadful place."

When Simba returned home, he found his friend Nala and her mother, Serafina, visiting with Sarabi. "Come on! I just heard about this great place!"

The mothers gave permission for the youngsters to go exploring, as long as Zazu went with them. Simba and Nala raced across the Pride Lands in an effort to lose the watchful bird. They led him through many herds of animals until they finally lost him.

Once the cubs were free of Zazu, Simba pounced on Nala, then Nala flipped Simba onto his back. They tumbled down a hill and landed in a dark ravine littered with elephant skulls and bones.

Simba looked around and gasped. "This is it! We made it!"

Before the cubs could explore any farther, Zazu tracked them down. "We're way beyond the boundary of the Pride Lands. And right now we are all in very real danger."

Suddenly, three hyenas slithered out of the eye sockets of an elephant skull. Frightened, Simba, Zazu, and Nala jumped back.

The hyenas, Banzai, Shenzi, and the always-laughing Ed, eyed them greedily.

Banzai sneered. "A trio of trespassers."

Zazu tried to lead the cubs to safety, but Banzai grabbed him by the neck and plopped him down. The hyenas circled their prey, licking their chops.

"What's the hurry? We'd love you to stick around for dinner."

　　While the hyenas argued about who was going to eat whom, Simba, Nala, and Zazu quietly slipped away. But the hyenas weren't distracted for long. They gave chase, and Simba and Nala had to run as fast as they could. Finally, they tried hiding behind some elephant bones.

　　Just when it looked as if it were all over for the young cubs, Mufasa appeared and sent the hyenas flying with a swipe of his big paw. "If you ever come near my son again ..."

　　The hyenas slinked away, and Mufasa glared at Simba.

　　"You deliberately disobeyed me! I'm very disappointed in you!"

Mufasa sent Nala and Zazu home so he could talk privately to his son. Simba peered up at his father.

"I was just trying to be brave, like you," he said.

"Being brave doesn't mean you go looking for trouble," said Mufasa. "Dad, we're pals, right? And we'll always be together, right?"

Mufasa looked up at the stars. "Simba, let me tell you something my father told me: Look at the stars. The great kings of the past look down on us from those stars. So whenever you feel alone, just remember that those kings will always be there to guide you. And so will I."

Meanwhile, the hyenas received another visitor: an angry Scar showed up at their lair. "I practically gift-wrapped those cubs and you couldn't even dispose of them."

Scar warned the hyenas to be prepared.

Banzai laughed. "Yeah! Be prepared. We'll be prepared! ... For what?"

Scar looked at him with danger in his eyes. "For the death of the king."

The following day, Scar invited Simba to join him in the gorge. When they arrived, Scar turned to his young nephew. "Now you wait here. Your father has a marvelous surprise for you."

Moments after he left, Scar signaled the hyenas, who chased a herd of wildebeests directly toward Simba.

From a distance, Mufasa noticed the rising dust. Scar appeared quickly at his side.

"Stampede! In the gorge! Simba's down there!"

Without waiting a second, Mufasa took off to save his young son.

Mufasa plunged into the gorge and battled his way through the oncoming wildebeests. He found Simba, grabbed him by the nape of his neck, and put him on a nearby ledge. Suddenly, Mufasa was knocked back into the stampede.

Desperately, he tried to climb up another ledge from which Scar stood looking down on him. "Brother—help me!" cried Mufasa.

Scar reached for Mufasa and pulled him close enough to whisper in his ear. "Long live the King." Then Scar let go of Mufasa and he fell to his death. Simba peered over the ridge just as his father disappeared beneath the thundering stampede.

Later, Scar found Simba hovering over his father's body, sobbing.
"It was an accident. I didn't mean for it to happen."

"But the king is dead," said Scar. "And if it weren't for you, he'd still
be alive. Oh, what will your mother think?"

Simba sobbed harder. "What am I going to do?"

"Run away, Simba. Run! Run away and never return."

Simba did as he was told, unaware that his uncle's hyena friends
had been ordered to finish him off. Scar returned to Pride Rock to
take over the throne.

Meanwhile, Simba plodded across the savannah without any food or water. It wasn't long before he fainted under the hot sun.

As the vultures circled overhead, a big-hearted warthog named Pumbaa stumbled upon the young lion. He turned to his trusty pal, a fast-talking meerkat named Timon. "He's so cute and all alone. Can we keep him?"

"Pumbaa, are you nuts? Lions eat guys like us." But Pumbaa scooped Simba up anyway and carried him to safety.

When Simba awoke, the first thought that sprang to mind was his father's death. Timon taught him about hakuna matata, which means no responsibilities, no worries.

"You've got to put your past behind you," Timon explained.

And that is exactly what Simba did. He stayed in the jungle with Pumbaa and Timon a long, long time, and grew into a very big lion. But eventually he became homesick. One night he looked up at the stars and recalled the words his father had told him long ago.

"The great kings of the past look down on us from those stars.

So, whenever you feel alone, just remember that those kings will always be there to guide you. And so will I."

The next day, Pumbaa was chased by a lioness.

Simba came to his rescue but, after wrestling with the lioness, who easily flipped him onto his back, he realized that she was his old friend. "Nala? What are you doing here?" he asked her.

"Why didn't you come back to Pride Rock? You're the king!" Nala replied.

"I'm not the king. Scar is."

"Simba, he let the hyenas take over the Pride Lands."

"What?"

"There's no food, no water. If you don't do something soon, everyone will starve. You're our only hope," Nala told him.

"I can't go back." Simba yelled at the heavens. He missed Mufasa terribly. "You said you'd always be there for me, but you're not ... because of me."

Simba didn't believe he could challenge Scar for the throne, so he stayed in the jungle with Nala and his new friends. But Rafiki knew the time had come for Simba to take his place in the Circle of Life, and he headed for the jungle.

When Simba saw Rafiki, he was surprised. "Who are you?"

"The question is: Who are you?" said Rafiki.

"I thought I knew. Now I'm not so sure," Simba replied.

"Well, I know who you are. You're Mufasa's boy. He's alive, and I'll show him to you. You follow old Rafiki. He knows the way."

Rafiki led Simba to a reflecting pool. When he looked into the water, he saw a lion. "That's not my father. It's just my reflection."

"Look harder ... You see, he lives in you."

The ghost of Mufasa magically appeared. "Look inside yourself, Simba. You are more than what you have become. You must take your place in the Circle of Life."

Encouraged by his father's words, Simba returned to Pride Rock. Nala, Pumbaa, and Timon followed. When Simba arrived, he found the land bare and dry. The hyenas were in control and Scar was shouting at Simba's mother.

Sarabi turned to Scar. "We must leave Pride Rock." She explained that there was no food left.

"We're not going anywhere. I am the king," said Scar.

"If you were half the king Mufasa was–"

"I AM TEN TIMES THE KING MUFASA WAS!"

Suddenly, a flash of lightning revealed the edge of Pride Rock, and there stood Simba. Scar jumped back.

"Simba ... I'm a little surprised to see you ... alive."

"Give me one good reason why I shouldn't rip you apart."

But Scar forced Simba to say, in front of all the lions, that he had caused his father's death.

Scar smirked. "Oh, Simba, you're in trouble again. But this time Daddy isn't here to save you. And now everyone knows why."

Simba backed up against the ledge. Lightning struck again, setting fire to the dry brush of the Pride Lands.

Simba leapt on Scar. Nala and the other lionesses joined the battle. Through the smoke and flames of the brushfire, Simba spotted Scar trying to escape and he ran after the old lion. Scar pleaded with his nephew. "Simba, I'll make it up to you. I promise. How can I prove myself to you?"

"Run. Run away, Scar, and never return."

Scar started to slink off, but then he turned and lunged one last time at Simba. Simba moved quickly and flipped Scar over the ledge, where a pack of hyenas was waiting hungrily.

Limping badly, Simba climbed up to the very top of Pride Rock. He let out a magnificent roar as he looked out over his kingdom.

Before long, Pride Rock flourished again. Nala remained by Simba's side, and soon they had their own newborn cub. With all their friends around, including Zazu, Pumbaa and Timon, a new celebration of life took place. After making a mark on the forehead of the young cub, Rafiki held him up for all the kingdom to see. The Circle of Life continued.

Three Little Fish

Three little fish,
Three little fish.
See how they swim,
See how they swim.
They all swam over the mermaid's tail,
And then leapt over the head of a whale!
Did you ever hear such a fabulous tale,
As three little fish?

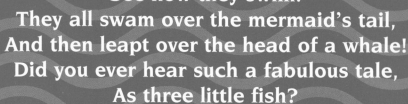

Sail Your Boat

Sail, sail, sail your boat,
Across the big blue sea.
If a mermaid swims your way,
Say hello from me!

Once upon a time, a little mermaid named Ariel frolicked below the ocean, exploring the hulls of sunken ships.

She beckoned to her playmate, a roly-poly fish. "Come on, Flounder! I'm sure this old boat has lots of human treasure aboard."

"I'm not g-g-going in there! It's spooky."

"Don't be such a guppy! Follow me!" Swimming inside the ship's cabin, Ariel discovered some rusted silverware. "Oh, my gosh! Have you ever seen anything so wonderful?"

Ariel swam to the water's surface and found her seagull friend. "Scuttle, do you know what this is?" She held up the fork.

"Judging from my expert knowledge of humans ... it's obviously a ... a dinglehopper! Humans use these to straighten their hair!"

"Thanks, Scuttle! It's perfect for my collection." Ariel dove to an undersea grotto, where she kept her treasures from the human world. She hid her collection there because her father, King Triton, forbade mer-people to have any contact with humans.

That night, Ariel saw strange lights shimmering over the ocean and swam up to investigate. On the surface she gaped at fireworks that flared above a large sailing ship. Scuttle soared down through the flickering colors. "Some celebration, huh, sweetie? It's the birthday of the human they call Prince Eric."

Forgetting her father's decree, Ariel peered at the young man on deck. "I've never seen a human this close. He's very handsome."

Aboard the ship, Eric's advisor, Sir Grimsby, motioned for the crew's attention. "It is now my privilege to present our esteemed prince with a very expensive, very large birthday gift–a marble statue carved in his exact likeness! ... Of course, I had hoped it would be a wedding present."

The prince glanced away, gazing at the sea. "Don't start, Grim. The right girl's out there ... somewhere ..."

Far beneath the ocean, the wicked sea witch, Ursula, used her magic to spy on Ariel. "My, my ... the daughter of the great sea king, Triton, in love with a human! A prince, no less. Her daddy will love that! Serves him right, that miserable old tyrant! Banishing me from his palace, just because I was a little ambitious. Still, this headstrong, lovesick girl may be the key to my revenge on Triton. She'll be the perfect bait—when I go fishing for her father!"

On the surface, a sudden storm whipped across the ocean. The prince took charge. "Stand fast! Secure the rigging!"

Without warning, a huge bolt of lightning struck the vessel.

Sir Grimsby slid across the deck. "Eric, look out! The mast is falling!"

Ariel watched in horror. "Eric's been knocked into the water! I've got to save him!"

With the storm swirling about her, Ariel desperately searched for Eric. "Where is he? If I don't find him soon—wait, there he is!"

Diving beneath the waves, Ariel spotted the unconscious figure. "He's sinking fast! I've got to pull him out of the water before he drowns!" She took hold of Eric and, using all her strength, managed to drag him to the surface.

As the storm died down, Ariel dragged the unconscious prince to shore. "He's still breathing! He must be alive."

A crab scuttled across the sand. It was Sebastian, Triton's music director. "Ariel, get away from that human! Your father forbids contact with them, remember?"

"But, Sebastian, why can't I stay with him? Why can't I be part of his world?" And she sang a haunting melody that voiced her longing to be with Eric forever.

A moment later, Ariel was back in the water, and Sir Grimsby was kneeling beside Eric. "You really delight in these sadistic strains on my blood pressure, don't you?"

"Grim, a girl rescued me ... She was singing in the most beautiful voice ..."

"I think you've swallowed a bit too much seawater! Here, Eric, let me help you to your feet."

Back at the palace, Triton noticed Ariel floating about as if in a dream. Summoning Sebastian, the sea king smiled. "You've been keeping something from me. I can tell Ariel's in love."

"I tried to stop her! I told her to stay away from humans!"
Sebastian blurted out before he realized what he was saying.
   "Humans!" Triton boomed angrily. "Ariel is in love with a human?"
   Triton found Ariel in her grotto. She was staring at Eric's statue,
which Flounder had retrieved after the storm.

"How many times have I told you to stay away from those fish-eating barbarians! Humans are dangerous!" Triton roared.

"But, Daddy, I love Eric!"

"So help me, Ariel, I am going to get through to you no matter what it takes!" Raising his trident, the sea king destroyed all her treasures. Then he stormed off, leaving Ariel in tears.

As she wept, two eels slithered up to her. "Don't be scared ...We represent someone who can help you!"

Ariel followed them to Ursula's den. "My dear, sweet child! I haven't seen you since your father banished me from his court! To show that I've reformed, I'll grant you three days as a human to win your prince. Before the sun sets on the third day, you must get him to kiss you. If you do, he's yours forever. But if you don't—you turn back into a mermaid and you belong to me!"

Ariel took a deep breath and nodded. The sea witch smiled deviously. "Oh yes, I almost forgot. We haven't discussed payment. I'm not asking much. All I want is—your voice!"

Sebastian, who had followed Ariel, scurried out of hiding. "Don't listen, Ariel! She is a demon!"

But Ursula had already used her powers to capture Ariel's beautiful voice in a seashell—and transform the little mermaid into a human!

Aided by Sebastian and Flounder, Ariel used her new legs to swim awkwardly to shore. There she found Prince Eric walking his dog. "Down, Max, down! I'm awfully sorry, miss."

Eric studied Ariel as she shied away from the animal.

"Hey, wait a minute. Don't I know you? Have ... have we ever met?"

Ariel opened her mouth to answer, forgetting that her voice was gone. The prince lowered his eyes. "You can't speak ... or sing, either? Then I guess we haven't met."

Eric gently took Ariel's arm. "Well, the least I can do is make amends for my dog's bad manners. C'mon, I'll take you to the palace and get you cleaned up."

At the royal estate, Ariel was whisked upstairs by Carlotta. Grimsby discovered the prince staring glumly out the window.

"Eric, be reasonable! Young ladies don't go around rescuing people ... then disappearing into thin air!"

"I'm telling you, she was real! If only I could find her ..."

The following afternoon, Eric took Ariel for a rowboat ride across a lagoon. Sebastian swam below them.

"Almost two days gone and that boy hasn't puckered up once! How is she going to get that boy to kiss her? Maybe this will help create the romantic mood."

He began conducting a sea creature chorus. " ... The music's working! Eric's leaning over to kiss Ariel."

As the prince bent toward her, the boat tipped and both Eric and Ariel fell into the water!

From her ocean lair, Ursula saw them tumble into the lagoon.
"That was too close for comfort! I can't let Ariel get away that easily!"

She began concocting a magic potion. "Soon Triton's daughter will be mine! Then I'll make the sea king writhe ... and wriggle like a worm on a hook!"

The next morning, Scuttle flew into Ariel's room in Eric's palace to congratulate her. The prince had announced his wedding!

Overjoyed at the news, Ariel hurried downstairs. She hid when she saw Eric introducing Grimsby to a mysterious dark-haired maiden. The prince seemed hypnotized.

"Vanessa saved my life. We're going to be married on board the ship at sunset."

Ariel drew back, confused. She was the one who had rescued Eric! Fighting tears, she fled the palace.

Sebastian found Ariel sitting on the dock, watching the wedding ship leave the harbor.

Suddenly, Scuttle crash-landed beside them. "When I flew over the boat, I saw Vanessa's reflection in a mirror! She's the sea witch—in disguise! And she's wearing the seashell containing Ariel's voice. We've got to stop the wedding!"

Sebastian splashed into the water. "Flounder, you help Ariel swim out to that boat! I'm going to get the sea king!"

Dripping wet, Ariel climbed aboard the ship just before sunset, as Eric and the maiden were about to be married.

Before Vanessa could say "I do," Scuttle and an army of his friends attacked her.

In the scuffle, the maiden's seashell necklace crashed to the deck, freeing Ariel's voice.

Suddenly, Vanessa sounded like the sea witch. "Eric, get away from her!"

Ariel smiled at the prince. "Oh Eric, I wanted to tell you ..."

Ursula grinned. "You're too late! The sun has set!"

Ariel felt her body changing back into a mermaid. As she dove into the water, the sea witch said, "You're mine, angelfish! But don't worry—you're merely the bait to catch your father! Why, here he is now!"

"I'll make a deal with you, Ursula—just don't harm my daughter!" Triton pleaded.

Instantly, Triton was changed into a tiny sea plant while Ariel watched. She stood heartbroken before Ursula, now queen of the ocean.

Suddenly, Prince Eric appeared. He tossed a harpoon at the sea witch, hitting her in the arm. Ursula snatched up the king's powerful trident. "You little fool!"

As the sea witch pointed the weapon at Eric, Ariel bumped into her, knocking the trident loose. "Eric, we have to get away from here!"

The moment they surfaced, huge tentacles shot out of the ocean. "Eric, we're surrounded. Look out!"

Ariel gasped as an enormous monster emerged. It was the sea witch! Using her new powers from the trident, Ursula turned the waters into a deadly whirlpool. Several old sunken ships rose to the surface.

The prince struggled aboard one of the boats. As Ursula loomed above Ariel, Eric plunged the sharp prow through the sea witch, destroying her. The mighty force sent Eric reeling toward shore.

As the unconscious prince lay on the beach, Ariel perched on a rock and gazed at him. Triton and Sebastian watched from afar.

"She really does love him, doesn't she, Sebastian?" The sea king waved his trident, and Ariel was once again human.

The next day, she and Prince Eric were married on board the wedding ship. As they kissed, the humans and mer-people sent up a happy cheer, linked at last by the marriage of two people whose love was as deep as the sea.

Toy Secrets

Woody sits on my bed,
He's my favorite toy.
He ropes and wrangles,
For he's a darin' cowboy.

He's buddies with Buzz,
Who watches for danger.
With lots of cool gear,
For he's a real space ranger.

My Toys

The toys on the bed jump up and down,
Up and down, up and down.
The toys on the bed jump up and down,
All through the day.

The trains on their tracks go clickety-clack,
Clickety-clack, clickety-clack.
The trains on their tracks go clickety-clack,
All through the day.

The blocks in the box all build and tumble,
Build and tumble, build and tumble.
The blocks in the box all build and tumble,
All through the day.

The dolls on the shelf all laugh and play,
Laugh and play, laugh and play.
The dolls on the shelf all laugh and play,
All through the day.

Every kid loves toys. Take Andy, for instance. He's got Rex the dinosaur, Hamm the piggy bank, Mr. Potato Head, Slinky Dog, and dozens of others. But his favorite toy is Woody, a cowboy doll who talks when Andy pulls his string.

"Reach for the sky! This town ain't big enough for the two of us."
You probably like your toys, too. But did you ever wonder what they
do when you leave the room? At Andy's house, the toys come alive!

One day, just before Andy's family was planning to move, Woody called the toys to order.

"Okay, first item today. Has everyone picked a moving buddy? I don't want any toys left behind. A moving buddy–if you don't have one, get one! Oh, yes, one minor note here. Andy's birthday party's been moved to today."

The toys gasped. The change of plans meant that today Andy would be getting new toys. And if Andy got new toys, he might throw his old ones away. Woody, sensing panic, tried to calm everyone down.

"I'm not worried. You shouldn't be worried," he said.

Then Hamm waddled up. "Birthday guests at three o'clock!"

At Woody's command, a group of toy soldiers hustled downstairs, carrying a baby monitor. Upstairs, the toys heard a soldier's voice through the speaker, describing Andy's presents. "The bow's coming off. We've got a lunchbox here. OK, second present . . . it appears to be . . . OK, it's bed sheets."

The toys seemed safe for another year. But there was one more surprise gift. "It's a huge package. Oh, wha–it's . . . it's–"

Rex bumped the speaker, and the batteries fell out. At the same time, there was a cheer from downstairs. The kids came racing upstairs to Andy's room as the toys scrambled back to their places.

Andy and his friends shoved Woody from his place on the bed and put a new toy there. They played with it, then raced back downstairs when it was time for games and prizes.

As the toys stirred, they heard a voice. "Buzz Lightyear to Star Command. Come in, Star Command. Why don't they answer?"

Woody climbed back up onto the bed and faced his worst fear: the coolest toy a kid could want, Buzz Lightyear.

He gulped. "There has been a bit of a mix-up. This is my spot, see, the bed here," Woody said to the new toy.

The other toys crowded around Buzz. Rex shook his hand. "Oh, I'm so glad you're not a dinosaur . . . Say! What's that button do?"

Buzz pressed the button, and wings popped out. All the toys were impressed—except for Woody. "These are plastic. He can't fly!"

"Yes, I can. Stand back, everyone. To infinity and beyond!"

Buzz leaped off the bed and headed straight for the floor. Then he bounced off a rubber ball and landed on a race car. The car took off on a track, spun through a loop, and bounced off a jump. Buzz flew out of the car, grabbing onto an airplane hung from the ceiling. After spinning around, he landed back on the bed. The toys cheered.

Woody couldn't believe it. "Well, in a couple of days, everything will be just the way it was. They'll see, I'm still Andy's favorite toy," he muttered.

Suddenly, the sound of barking interrupted the toys. They rushed to the window. It was Scud, the dog next door. With him was Sid, his owner, a kid who loved to torture toys.

Rex shook his head. "Oh, no. I can't bear to watch one of these again." As the toys looked on helplessly, Sid strapped a firecracker to his Combat Carl toy, lit the fuse, and blew the toy to smithereens.

Sid cheered. "Yes! He's gone! He's history. That was very sweet. Did you see that, Scud?"

Bo Peep turned away. "The sooner we move, the better."

Late that afternoon, the family finished packing boxes. Andy's mum told him they were going to Pizza Planet, his favorite restaurant, for the last time. She said he could bring one toy. Woody, who was listening, knew it would be either him or Buzz.

Seeing a space between the edge of the desk and the wall, Woody got an idea.

"Buzz . . . Buzz Lightyear, we've got trouble! A helpless toy–it's, it's trapped, Buzz!"

As Buzz leaned over the edge, Woody steered a remote control car toward him. Buzz dove out of the way, but the desk lamp swung around and accidentally knocked him out the window!

Mr. Potato Head saw it all. "Couldn't handle Buzz cutting in on your playtime, could you, Woody? Didn't want to face the fact that Buzz just might be Andy's new favorite toy, so you got rid of him."

"No! Wait! I can explain everything."

Woody never had the chance because just then Andy came into the room. "Mum, do you know where Buzz is?"

"Just grab some other toy. Now, come on."

"OK." Andy picked up Woody and carried him out to the van, past the bush where Buzz had landed. Buzz, seeing Andy take Woody into the van, raced after it and hopped on the back bumper.

The van pulled into a gas station and Andy got out, leaving Woody on the back seat. Woody looked up and saw Buzz, covered with mud, staring at him through the sunroof. "I just want you to know that even though you tried to terminate me, revenge is not an idea we promote on my planet."

Woody sighed with relief. "Oh. Oh, that's good."

"But we're not on my planet, are we?" Buzz lunged for Woody.

The two of them fell off the seat, out the open door, and rolled under the van. They were still on the ground, fighting, when the door slid shut and the van drove away.

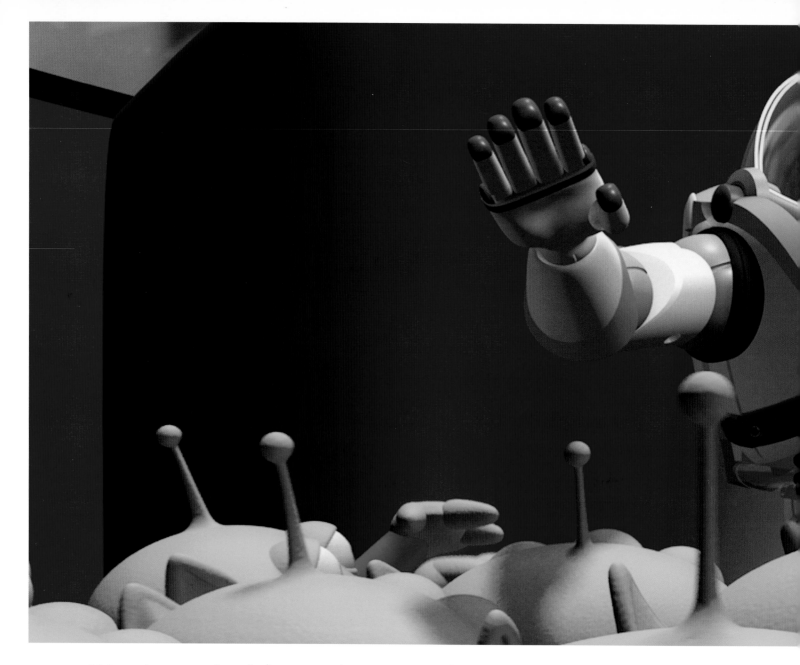

Woody watched the van leave. "I'm lost! Oh, I'm a lost toy."

Buzz was upset for a different reason. "And you, my friend, are responsible for delaying my rendezvous with Star Command."

"YOU-ARE-A-TOY! You aren't the real Buzz Lightyear; you're … you're an action figure. You are a CHILD'S PLAYTHING!"

Buzz shook his head. "You are a sad, strange little man, and you have my pity. Farewell."

As Buzz walked off, a Pizza Planet delivery truck with a plastic rocket on its roof pulled into the station. Woody had an idea. "Buzz! I found a spaceship!"

Buzz peered inside the truck.

"Now, you're sure this space freighter will return to its port of origin once it jettisons its food supply?"

Woody nodded. "Uh-huh. And when we get there, we'll be able to find a way to transport you home."

Sure enough, the truck took them to its port of origin–Pizza Planet. Buzz looked around in amazement. "What a spaceport!"

Then Woody spotted Andy with his mum and baby sister, Molly. Seeing a basket on Molly's stroller, Woody grinned. "OK, when I say go, we're going to jump in the basket." But Buzz was gone.

Buzz had spotted a game shaped like a rocket, and thought it might take him home. Inside, he found himself surrounded by squeeze-toy aliens.

"I am Buzz Lightyear. Who's in charge here?"

The aliens pointed up at a giant crane. "The claw is our master. The claw chooses who will go and who will stay. Shhhh! It moves."

Woody, who had followed Buzz into the game, gazed up in horror. "Oh, no! Sid!" Andy's cruel neighbor was at the controls.

The claw came down. It grabbed Buzz and pulled him upward. Woody clung to his legs, desperately trying to pull him free.

Sid was thrilled. "All right! Double prizes!"

Sid raced home with Woody and Buzz in his backpack. He tossed the pack onto his bed, shut the door, and went downstairs.

Woody got out of the pack, ran across the bed, and leaped onto the doorknob. "Locked! There's got to be another way out of here."

There was a noise behind him, and a doll's head looked out from under the bed. Woody smiled. "Hi there, little fella. Come out here. Do you know a way out of here?"

The head continued toward him, propelled by a creepy, spider-like body made from the pieces of an Erector set. In horror, Woody scrambled back up onto the bed. "B-B-B-Buzz!"

The doll was joined by other mutant toys assembled from parts of different toys by Sid. Woody jumped inside the backpack and Buzz zipped it shut, punching a button on his chest. "Mayday! Mayday! Come in Star Command! Send reinforcements!"

He adjusted his laser light and turned to Woody.

"I've set my laser from stun to kill."

"Yeah, and if anyone attacks us we can blink 'em to death."

But instead of attacking, the mutant toys crept back out of sight. Woody and Buzz were safe . . . for the time being, at least.

The next morning, when Sid went downstairs, Woody jumped to his feet. "The door–it's open! We're free!"

He and Buzz raced for the hallway, but their path was blocked by the mutant toys. As the monsters approached, Buzz turned to Woody. "Shield your eyes!" He fired his laser. Nothing happened.

Woody shook his head in disgust. "Oh, you idiot–you're a TOY! Use your karate chop action!"

Woody pushed a button on Buzz's back and Buzz's arms began chopping. The mutant toys backed away, giving Woody and Buzz room to slip through the door.

While Woody was scouting the hallway, Buzz ducked inside another room. Behind him, a voice rang out. "Calling Buzz Lightyear. This is Star Command." The voice was coming from a commercial on TV, advertising Buzz Lightyear toys. Woody had been right after all.

Buzz was just a toy. Stunned, Buzz staggered to the top of the stairs. He opened his wings and jumped, hoping to fly. Instead, he crashed to the floor.

By the time Woody found him, Buzz had been discovered by Sid's sister, Hannah. She had dressed him up for a tea party and given him a new name. "Would you like some tea, Mrs. Nesbit?"

When Hannah left the room, Woody ran inside. He found Buzz with one arm. "Look at me. I can't even fly out of a window."

Woody smiled. "Out the window . . . Buzz, you're a genius!"

He dragged Buzz back into Sid's room, then stood in the window and called to the toys in Andy's room across the way. "Hey, guys! Guys! Hey!"

When the toys appeared, Buzz wouldn't help. So Woody picked up Buzz's arm and waved it, as if Buzz were standing behind the window frame. "Hiya, fellas. To infinity and beyond!"

But Woody held the arm too high, and Mr. Potato Head saw that it had been broken off. "Murderer! You murdering dog!"

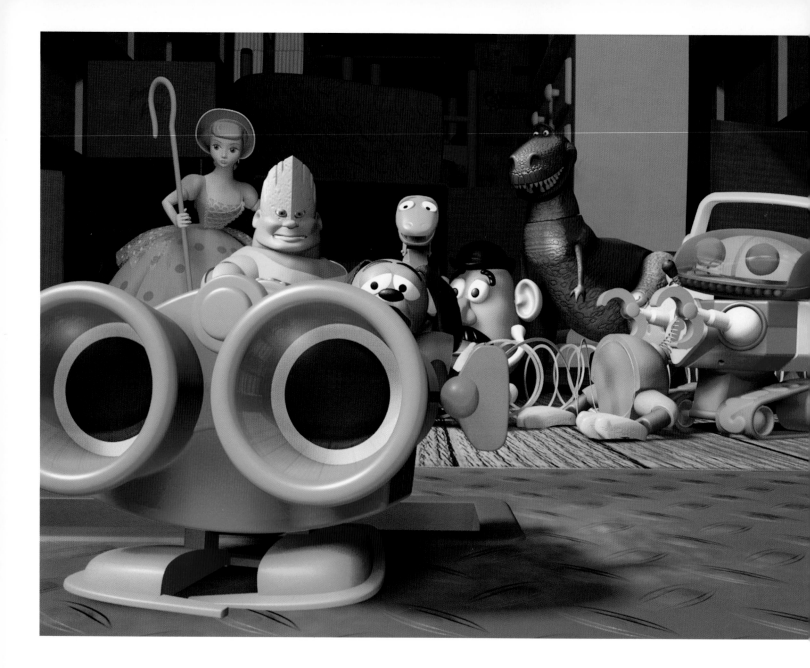

Once again, the toys believed that Woody had done something awful to Buzz. As they hurried away from the window, Woody tried to stop them. "You've got to help us, please! You don't know what it's like over here!"

But it was no use. Before Woody could turn around, the mutants were all over Buzz.

Woody tried to stop them. "All right, back! Back, you cannibals!"

But the toys grabbed Buzz's arm and pushed Woody aside.

When they backed away, Buzz's arm was in place! Woody couldn't believe it. "Hey! Hey, they fixed you!" He tried to thank the mutant toys, but they scrambled back under the bed.

Sid came into the room with a brand-new rocket. "What am I going to blow? Man . . . hey, where's that wimpy cowboy doll?"

As Woody hid under a milk crate, Sid spotted Buzz. He set his tool box on the crate, trapping Woody. Then he picked up Buzz and taped the rocket to his back. "Yes! To infinity and beyond!"

There was a clap of thunder, and it started to rain. Sid looked outside. "Aw, man." He sat at the window, waiting for it to stop.

Sid wasn't the only one hoping for sunshine. Next door, Andy and his mum had finished packing for their move the next day.

Andy went to bed, sad that he never found his favorite toys.

While Andy and Sid slept, Woody called to Buzz for help. Buzz lay with the rocket on his back, too sad to move. "I'm just a toy."

Woody glared at him. "Look, over in that house is a kid who thinks you are the greatest and it's not because you're a space ranger, pal. It's because you're a toy. You are his toy!"

A few moments later, the crate began to shake. Buzz was trying to push the tool box off! "Come on, sheriff. There's a kid over in that house who needs us. Now, let's get you out of this thing!"

Just as Buzz managed to free Woody, Sid's alarm clock rang.

Sid jumped out of bed, grabbed Buzz, and headed outside.

As Sid's toys crept out from under the bed, Woody asked them for help. "Please, he's my friend, he's the only one I've got." The toys gathered around. "OK, I think I know what to do, and if it works, it'll help everybody."

Working together, they escaped to the backyard, where Sid was starting to light the rocket. Suddenly he saw Woody lying nearby. "Hey! How'd you get out here?"

As Sid watched, an army of mutant toys rose from the grass and marched toward him. Woody grinned. "From now on, you must take good care of your toys. Because if you don't, we'll find out, Sid."

Sid ran screaming into the house.

As Woody rushed to help Buzz, a car horn honked. Next door, Andy's family and their moving truck were leaving. Buzz, with the rocket still strapped to his back, motioned to Woody. "Come on!"

They raced after the truck and grabbed onto the back. Woody held on, but Buzz fell to the street. "Buzz!"

Thinking fast, Woody found Andy's toy box inside the moving van and dug out the remote-controlled car. He tossed it into the street and steered it toward Buzz, who got on.

Mr. Potato Head, thinking Woody was trying to get rid of another toy, called to the others. "Get him! Toss him overboard!"

"No, no, wait!" But they pushed Woody into the street.

Woody bounced off the pavement and onto the car, right next to Buzz. They chased after the van in the remote-controlled car. But the batteries ran out, and it slowed to a stop.

Woody looked around. Seeing the sun through Buzz's helmet, he used it to focus sunlight on the rocket fuse. When the fuse lit, Woody grabbed Buzz, and they rocketed toward the moving truck, soaring in the air—but missed!

Buzz popped open his wings, tearing away the rocket from his back. The two of them glided over Andy's van towards Andy's mom's car. "Hey, Buzz! You're flying!"

They dipped through the sunroof and into an open box next to Andy. He let out a happy yell. "Hey! Wow! Woody! Buzz!"

A few months later, Woody, Buzz, and the other toys were gathered around the baby monitor once again. It was their first Christmas in the new house, and Andy was opening his presents.

Woody smiled. "Buzz Lightyear, you're not worried, are you?"
"Me? No, no. Are you?"
"Now, Buzz, what could Andy possibly get that is worse than you?"
Woody and Buzz looked at each other. Downstairs, they heard
Andy yell, "It's a puppy!"

Dilly, Dilly

Rubies are red, dilly, dilly,
Emeralds are green.
When I am Sultan, dilly, dilly
You shall be queen.

The Magic Lamp

Aladdin once found a magic lamp,
that had lost its golden glow.
It lay in the Cave of Wonders
Where thieves did come and go

With a gentle polish and a little rub
Aladdin soon made a genie appear
"I've been in that lamp too long," he said.
"I grant you three wishes, do you hear?"

Aladdin couldn't believe his luck
And wondered what he should do
He asked if he could become a prince
And then his wishes were down to two

Aladdin was kidnapped by the evil Jafar
But was saved by the genie and his magic
He gave him his last wish as thanks
For without him, the end would be tragic.

DISNEY'S *Aladdin*

On a starry moonlit night, a dark figure named Jafar led a shifty thief to a secret cave in the desert.

When the magnificent carved head of a tiger rose out of the sand and revealed the entrance to the cave, Jafar ordered the thief inside. "Bring me the lamp. The rest of the treasure is yours—but the lamp is mine."

The tiger head stopped the thief.

"Know this. Only one whose rags hide a heart that's pure may enter here ... the Diamond in the Rough."

Jafar turned to his parrot companion, Iago.

"I must find this one ... this 'Diamond in the Rough'."

Far away in the marketplace of Agrabah, a young man in ragged clothes ran for his life after stealing a loaf of bread. The boy, whose name was Aladdin, escaped with the help of his pet monkey and sidekick, Abu. Sitting on the rooftop with the stale bread, Aladdin looked around sadly at their meagre surroundings.

"Someday, Abu, things are gonna change. We'll be dressed in robes instead of rags ... and be inside a palace looking out ... instead of outside looking in."

Nearby, in the garden of the royal palace, the Sultan worried that his daughter, Princess Jasmine, wouldn't like her latest suitor.

"Dearest, you've got to stop rejecting every man who comes to call. The law says you must marry a prince by your next birthday."

Jasmine sadly petted her pet tiger, Rajah. "Papa, if I do marry, I want it to be for love."

Later that night, with only three days left until her next birthday, Jasmine slipped out over the garden wall, to escape the pressures of palace life.

She had never ventured past the palace walls before so she was unsure what to expect.

Unaware that the royal vizier, Jafar, was secretly plotting to take control of the kingdom, the Sultan tried to consult with his advisor about his daughter. But avoiding the Sultan, Jafar retreated to his laboratory to work on his plan. While concocting a spell, a lightning bolt suddenly hit his hourglass and an image of Aladdin appeared. Jafar was surprised to discover that Aladdin was the Diamond in the Rough, able to enter the cave and retrieve the lamp. "Iago, have the guard, Rasoul, find this boy and escort him to the palace."

Free at last, Jasmine wandered through her new world, disguised and dazzled by the sights and sounds of the marketplace.

When she innocently took an apple to feed a hungry boy, the cart owner screamed: "Thief!"

Unaware that she was a princess, Aladdin rushed in to rescue her. "You're new to the marketplace. Where are you from?"

"What does it matter ... I ran away, and I am not going back."

Suddenly Rasoul grabbed Aladdin. Jasmine turned angrily to the palace guard. "Unhand him—by order of the princess."

Stunned to learn her true identity, Aladdin could only look back helplessly as Rasoul, following Jafar's orders, hauled him away.

While Jasmine mourned losing Aladdin, Abu found him chained in a dark dungeon thinking only of her.

Jafar, disguised as a prisoner, limped towards Aladdin.

"I know where there is a cave, boy, with enough treasure to impress even the lovely princess. I need a young pair of legs and a strong back to go in after it."

"I would gladly help, sir, but how do we get out of here?"

Jafar moved a stone and a hidden staircase was revealed.

Moments later they were making their way across the desert.

Jafar led Aladdin and Abu to the Cave of Wonders. This time, the tiger's head at the mouth of the cave allowed Aladdin to enter. Jafar called in after Aladdin. "Remember, first bring me the lamp. Then you may touch the treasure, but not before."

Inside, Aladdin and Abu discovered a huge cavern filled with riches. "Would you look at that? Why, just a handful of this stuff would make us richer than the Sultan." It was difficult for Abu to keep from grabbing the fortune before them.

As Abu and Aladdin explored the cave, a golden-tassled carpet came to life and played peek-a-boo with them. "Look, Abu, a magic carpet!" The carpet floated closer. "Your owner must have come looking for the lamp, too. Do you know where it is?" The carpet zipped off to reveal a huge cavern. The lamp rested at the top of a high stone staircase. While Aladdin climbed, Abu eyed a monkey idol holding a huge jewel nearby. Just as Aladdin reached the lamp, Abu grabbed the jewel. Instantly the voice of the tiger's head echoed through the chamber: "You have touched the forbidden treasure! Now you shall never again see the light of day!"

The cavern shook violently and the piles of treasure transformed into mountains of fire. Aladdin, Abu and the carpet scrambled to escape. At the cave's entrance, Iago squawked. From above, Jafar reached down to grab Aladdin's hand. "First give me the lamp." When Aladdin did, Jafar clutched the lamp and quickly hid it under his robe. Then he released Aladdin and brushed Abu off his cloak, sending them hurtling back into the cave. "It's mine! It's all mine! With the power of this lamp I will control the kingdom." But when Jafar reached back into his robe for the lamp–it was gone!

The Magic Carpet caught the tumbling duo as the cave entrance closed and everything became still. Chattering excitedly, Abu happily revealed the lamp. Aladdin laughed.

"Abu, why, you little thief." Aladdin rubbed some dirt off the lamp to get a better look. Colorful smoke spewed out of the spout and it took the form of a gigantic Genie! "Say, you're a lot smaller than my last master." Aladdin was stunned.

"Wait a minute," said Aladdin. "I'm your master?"

"That's right. Direct from the lamp! Right here for your wish fulfilment. Three wishes to be exact. Uno. Dos. Tres." In a dazzling display the Genie demonstrated his magical powers.

Aladdin cleverly tricked the Genie into rescuing them from the cave without using up a wish. Then he smiled at his newfound friend. "Genie, if you could have a wish, what would you wish for?"

"To be my own master! Such a thing would be greater than all the magic and all the treasures in all the world."

"I'll do it. I'll set you free. I'll use my third wish to set you free."

The Genie was delighted. "Let's make some magic. What is it you want most?"

"Well, could you make me a prince?" asked Aladdin.

In a flash, the Genie created elegant robes and servants for Aladdin and turned him into Prince Ali.

Back at the palace, Jafar and Iago discussed what to do next.
Iago had an idea. "Marry the princess and you become the Sultan."
Jafar thought about it. "The idea has merit." Excited, he went to see
the Sultan. Unrolling an official-looking scroll, Jafar read out loud:
"If the princess has not chosen a husband by her next birthday, then
the Sultan shall choose for her. And, in the event a suitable prince
cannot be found, the princess may wed the royal vizier. That's me."

Using his snake-eyed staff to hypnotise the Sultan, Jafar ordered
him to arrange the marriage.

Dressed as Prince Ali, Aladdin rode triumphantly through the Agrabah bazaar atop Abu, who had been transformed into an elephant. Wearing elegant robes and surrounded by an entourage of dancers, swordsmen and attendants, he swept through the palace gates.

The Sultan greeted him enthusiastically. "Oh, I'm sure Jasmine will like this one."

Jasmine, however, thought her father was trying to marry her off again and she became angry and stomped off. Aladdin was crestfallen and the Genie offered his wisdom. "Be yourself, Al."

Aladdin went after the princess and floated up to her balcony on the Magic Carpet.

This time she looked at him more closely. "Wait, have we met before? You remind me of someone I saw in the marketplace." Jasmine moved to the balcony railing. Aladdin smiled.

"It's a Magic Carpet. Would you like to go for a ride?" he asked her.

Hesitantly, Jasmine took Aladdin's hand and stepped onto the Carpet. The Carpet whisked them off. Slightly startled, Jasmine threw her arms around Aladdin. Below them was a breathtaking view of the palace and the city in the moonlight.

During the flight, Jasmine looked more closely at Aladdin.

"You are the boy from the market. I knew it. Why did you lie to me?" Aladdin nervously answered. "The truth is I sometimes dress as a commoner, but I really am a prince."

When the magical ride ended, the Carpet zipped back to the palace. Fireworks exploded and Jasmine reached out for Aladdin's hand.

As he helped her onto the balcony, they looked into each other's eyes. Impatient, the Carpet bumped Aladdin into a kiss with Jasmine.

Aladdin beamed. "Sleep well, Princess."

Jasmine looked into his eyes. "Good night, my handsome prince."

Jafar was afraid that his plot to marry Jasmine and become Sultan would be ruined by Aladdin, so he ordered Rasoul to kidnap the boy and throw him from a high cliff into the water. Nearly drowning, Aladdin feebly reached for the lamp. When the Genie appeared, he saw it was no joking matter.

"You have to say 'Genie, I want you to save my life'."

Aladdin nodded.

The Genie said, "I'll take that as a yes."

The Genie granted Aladdin's second wish by using his magic to swiftly take them both to the surface.

At the palace, Jasmine rushed happily to see her father.

"Oh, Papa! I just had the most wonderful time. I have some good news for you."

The Sultan, still under Jafar's spell, looked at his daughter. "So do I, Jasmine ... I have chosen a husband for you. You will wed Jafar."

Jasmine turned angrily to Jafar. "I will never marry you. I choose Prince Ali."

Jafar laughed. "Prince Ali left ... like all the others."

Suddenly Aladdin, still dressed as the prince, appeared in the doorway and exposed Jafar as a traitor.

When Aladdin returned to his room the Genie happily popped out of the lamp. "Hail the conquering hero! Aladdin! You've just won the heart of the princess! What are you going to do next?"

The Genie waited while Aladdin scowled. "I'm sorry, Genie. I can't free you.

I can't let Jasmine find out that I'm not really a prince. I need to keep my third wish."

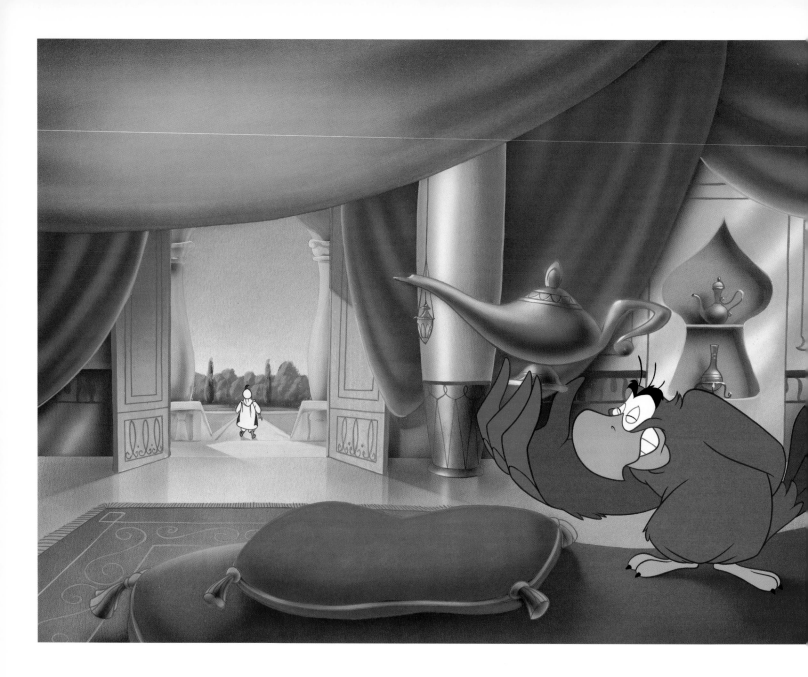

Disappointed, the Genie disappeared back into his lamp.

Iago flew into the room and, while Aladdin went outside, the parrot stole the lamp.

Jafar greedily rubbed the stolen lamp. When the Genie appeared, Jafar yanked him up close. "I am your master now. Grant my first wish! I wish to be Sultan!" Using his powers, the Genie had no choice and transformed Jafar's clothing into the Sultan's robes.

But when Jafar appeared before Aladdin and Jasmine as the Sultan, they refused to obey him.

Jafar turned to the Genie. "For my second wish, I wish to be the most powerful sorcerer in the world." The Genie nodded sadly and granted the wish. Then with his sorcerer's powers, Jafar transformed Aladdin's princely robes back into rags. "Look at your prince now!" he said to Jasmine.

Aladdin looked sadly at the princess. "Jasmine, I'm sorry."

Eager to be rid of Aladdin, Jafar trapped the boy and his friends in a tower and zapped it to the ends of the earth. Bewildered, Aladdin crawled out of a snow bank and turned to Abu. "This is all my fault! I should have freed the Genie when I had the chance. I'm sorry. I made a mess of everything. I've got to go back and set things right."

Aladdin quickly rescued the Carpet from beneath the fallen tower and was swept aboard. Together, Aladdin and Abu soared up over the clouds back towards Agrabah.

Back at the palace, Jafar sat majestically on the throne.

Just when it looked like Jafar was about to have everything he wanted, Aladdin reappeared.

Jafar knocked Aladdin backwards and zapped Jasmine inside a giant hourglass. "You thought you could outwit the most powerful being on earth? Without the Genie, boy, you're nothing."

Aladdin thought of a way to finally be rid of Jafar. "That may be true, but the Genie has more power than you'll ever have." Shocked at the thought, Jafar got an idea.

"I'm ready to make my third wish!" cried Jafar. "I wish to be a Genie."

Magical energy swirled around Jafar as he was transformed into a Genie. Jafar cried out gleefully. "The universe is mine to command!"

Aladdin picked up the lamp and smiled. "You wanted to be a Genie? You got it! And everything that goes with it." Suddenly, large gold cuffs clamped onto Jafar's wrists and a lamp took shape. Jafar reached out and grabbed Iago's feet as they both vanished inside the lamp.

The Genie laughed and clapped Aladdin on the back. Everything changed by Jafar's magic was restored to normal as the Genie hurled the lamp back to the Cave of Wonders with Jafar inside.

Aladdin and Jasmine stood on the balcony. "Jasmine, I'm sorry that I lied to you about being a prince," Aladdin told her.

The Genie appeared beside them. "No problem, you've still got one wish left. Just say the word and you're a prince again."

"No, it's time I started keeping my promises. Genie, I wish for your freedom."

The cuffs vanished from the stunned Genie's wrists.

The Sultan smiled. "You've certainly proved your worth to me. I declare that the princess shall marry whomever she deems worthy."

Jasmine leapt into Aladdin's arms. "Aladdin, I choose you."

As Aladdin and Jasmine kissed, a happy Genie disappeared into the sky to enjoy his new-found freedom.